Tales to Tell

Diagnosis

Stephen Comer

Dark Imagination Entertainment

Author – [Stephen Comer]

Illustrations by [Juaquin Guerra]

[First] edition [2025]

ISBN – [979-8-9996916-2-0]

Contents

This book is dedicated to Dennis Comer. He was a great man and an even better father. He has been the biggest inspiration to me and who I want to be in the future. I will do all that I can to hopefully continue making him proud in the afterlife. My dad always said "Be Somebody!" and that's exactly what I am going to try to do.

Chapter 1

A Cut Too Deep

I had just finished my dinner. I was reluctant to eat, though—I had the worst headache and felt nauseous for most of the day. Still, I knew my rumbling stomach needed it.

I got up from the dining room table and carefully carried the delicate porcelain plate toward the sink. As I walked, the entire left side of my body suddenly felt weak, as if a weight were pulling me down. Despite my best efforts to hold onto the plate, I fell to the floor, and the plate shattered into pieces upon impact.

Instinctively, my hands shot out, grasping for stability where none remained. The razor-sharp edges of broken ceramic met soft flesh—a searing kiss that bloomed into crimson. A gasp escaped my lips—not so much from the pain, but from the sheer abruptness of it all. The plate, my dinner, the simple act of clearing the table—everything had become part of an unexpected, violent little drama.

I tried to get up, but I was frozen. Minutes passed before the muscles on the left side of my body suddenly came back to life. I scrambled to my feet, leaving a faint red trail across the linoleum as I rushed to the kitchen sink. The dishcloth—damp and faintly scented with soap—became a makeshift bandage, a clumsy attempt to stanch the bleeding.

Panic slithered in, cold and tight around my chest. This wasn't just a cut—I could feel it in the persistent throb, the warmth spreading beneath the cloth, the way the fabric darkened too quickly. I held my hand over the sink, anguished and in pain.

The decision was immediate: the emergency room.

My keys, hanging innocently by the door, suddenly felt weighty—charged with the urgency of the moment. The short drive was a blur of adrenaline and mounting unease. Each red light mocked my haste; each passing car felt like an obstacle between me and relief.

The sterile scent of antiseptic thickened the air in the waiting room—a jarring contrast to the warmth of home. Time slowed. Each minute stretched, bloated with tension. The television droned in the background, its cheerful, hollow chatter a cruel counterpoint to the turmoil roiling within me.

At the emergency desk of the Buster Memorial Hospital sat an older woman with bags under her eyes but the energy of a teenager. I explained my situation, and she said it sounded like a possible stroke. They'd set me up in a room, she assured me, and Dr. Bachman would be in to see me as soon as possible.

The examination room was small and impersonal—the fluorescent lights too bright, the silence too loud. Two framed certificates hung on the wall. Both bore the name *Dr. Stephen*

Bachman—one a doctorate in Psychology, the other in Neurology.

Then Dr. Bachman entered.

His voice was disembodied, clinical, yet laced with hope.

He had the look of professionalism—and something out of a sci-fi novel. His blonde hair was slicked back, combed to perfection, and a monocle magnified one eye, which held an unsettling depth. He moved with a slight hitch in his step, a sleek black cane assisting his gait.

"If you don't mind me asking... what's with the cane?" I said, second-guessing my curiosity.

Dr. Bachman gave a small shrug. "Old injury," he said. "Bad leg. Acts up sometimes, so I occasionally need it."

I nodded, unsure of what to say next. He didn't offer more, and I didn't press.

He turned to my hand, his touch surprisingly gentle as he unwrapped the blood-soaked cloth.

His brow furrowed as he examined the wound.

"So," he said, looking up, "what brings you in tonight?"

I recounted the details. He listened without interruption, his expression unreadable—eyes sharp and quiet.

The stitching was a ritual—precise, practiced, efficient. He worked in silence, occasionally breaking it with small talk. Questions about my life. My hobbies. My past.

"Any sports when you were younger?" he asked, his tone casual.

I told him about my teenage dedication—how athleticism had once defined me, how pressure and burnout had followed. He nodded thoughtfully, his gaze drifting for a moment as if assembling the edges of a puzzle I couldn't yet see.

Then he asked, "Has your body ever done anything like what your leg did tonight?"

I told him yes, but nothing like tonight—this was different. Those times had been minor, barely noticeable, so I never thought much of it. I just chalked it up to all the years of playing football. I figured it was my age finally catching up with me.

Then came the unexpected request.

"I'd like to run a few tests," Dr. Bachman said matter-of-factly. "Just a standard precaution. From everything you've said, it sounds like a possible stroke."

The tests varied. I received a CT scan, CT angiography, and some blood work—and oh boy, did I hate needles. It's not like I was a wuss, but really, who likes being stabbed by a stranger?

"Is that really necessary?" I asked, skepticism threading through my voice.

"Your whole left side went numb, Mr. Henson. This is very serious," he replied, his tone firm but courteous. "We just want to be thorough."

Reluctantly, I agreed. Maybe I was just worried about what the results might be. Still, I was sure I was fine.

The nurse walked in with everything prepared for the blood draw. The needle felt cold, somehow alien, as it filled the vial. Dr. Bachman left the room, his black cane tapping softly against the hard floor.

After the blood draw was finished, it was another twenty minutes before I was taken back for the CT scan and angiography. It was late, and I was tired.

Was I worried? Sure, I was. But I hoped everything would be fine.

There were so many things running through my mind that night. The heaviest of them all was the loss of my father. He had suffered from Multiple Sclerosis, and a few months after his diagnosis, he tragically passed from a stroke.

Not long before that, my mother had passed away too. Would that be the same fate for me? I wasn't sure—but it was impossible not to think about it.

After all the tests were complete, I was brought back into the room. I lay there in bed, the thoughts still racing in my head.

Eventually, my eyes began to close.

And I fell into a deep sleep.

An hour later, I was awakened by the sound of Dr. Bachman walking into the room and clearing his throat.

"Well, Mr. Henson, I went through all the results. There's no sign of anything indicating this was a stroke," he said in a disappointed tone.

Confused, I asked, "Why do you sound disappointed? That's good news... right?"

He responded, "Technically, yes. But on the other hand, it could be something worse. I'm not trying to scare or worry you, Mike, but someone's body doesn't just do that for no reason."

I could tell he wasn't trying to alarm me, but I was a little worried now. So I asked, "What's next?"

He began asking about my medical history—if I or any family members had known health conditions.

I told him I didn't, then mentioned my teenage years and my father's passing after being diagnosed with MS. His expression shifted, concerned. He asked why I hadn't mentioned that earlier.

"I didn't think it was relevant," I said. "Or maybe... maybe I just didn't want to believe something was truly wrong with me."

He nodded solemnly. "MS isn't necessarily hereditary, but there is a genetic component. You should've brought this up."

I apologized. "I didn't even think about it."

He told me more tests would be necessary to rule out the possibility of MS. I told him how exhausted I felt, and he agreed to let me rest and run the tests in the morning.

After he left the room, I laid there, too overwhelmed to fall back asleep. The weight of it all pressed down on me. I didn't know how to process the situation. I didn't want to suffer the same fate as my father—not yet, not like this.

Thirty minutes later, I finally drifted off again.

The next morning, my best friend Jack—assistant manager at Hondel Co., where we both worked—showed up before the tests. Apparently, I had called him sometime during the night to say I wouldn't be making it to work. I had no recollection of the call. Maybe it was the lack of sleep or the crushing stress. I hadn't told him what the tests were for. I didn't want to worry him—or risk missing more days at work.

I underwent several tests, the worst being the spinal tap. I was reluctant, but at this point, I had to know what had happened to me. What was wrong with me? What I'd hoped was nothing now seemed like it could be something far worse.

After the long series of tests, while Jack was down in the cafeteria, Dr. Bachman returned.

He told me he'd need to go through my full medical history—especially old injuries from my football days—and conduct a thorough investigation before he could give me a definitive diagnosis. He scheduled a follow-up appointment for the following week.

Once Dr. Bachman left, Jack came back into the room. I told him we were good to go.

Then I headed home—to get some much-needed rest.

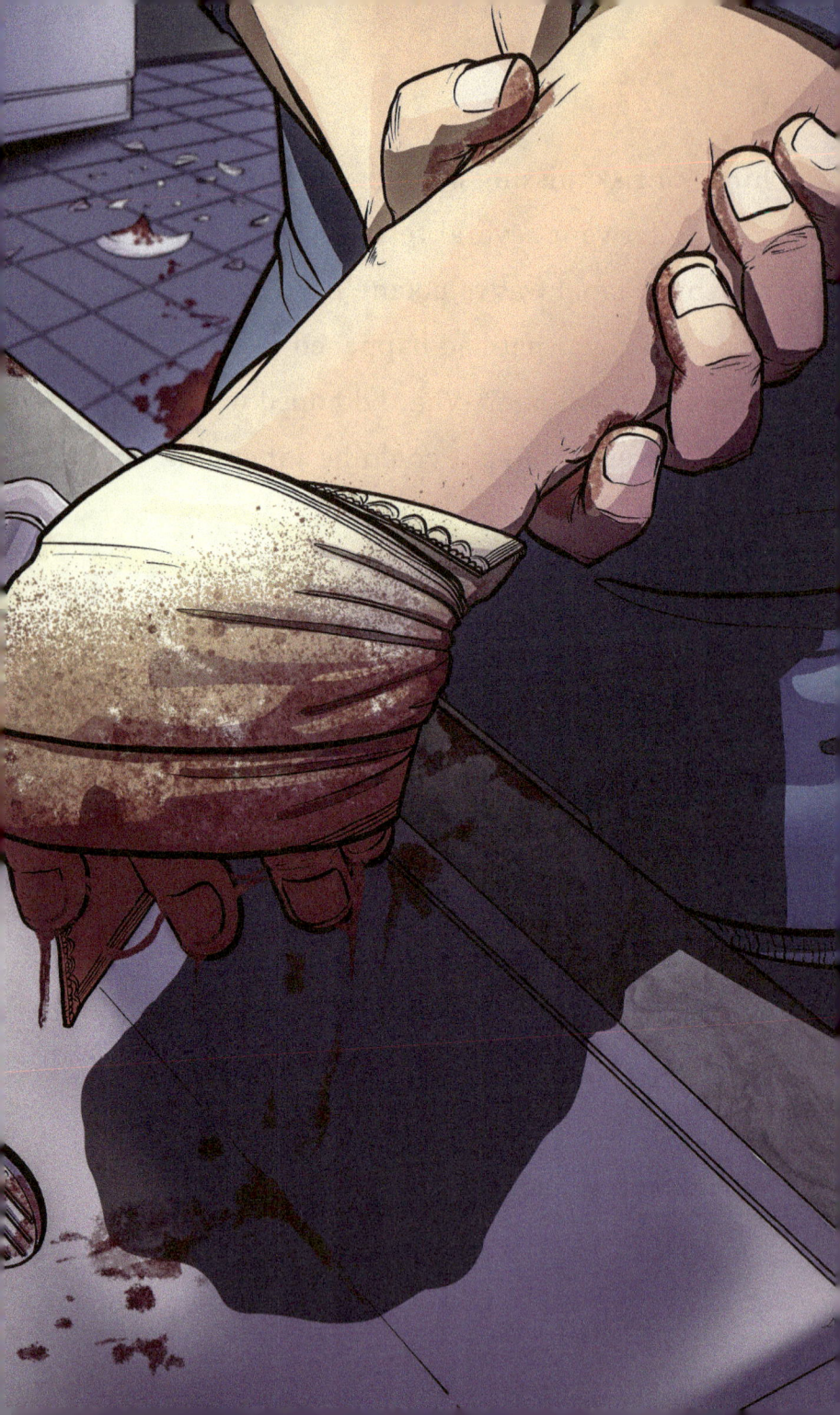

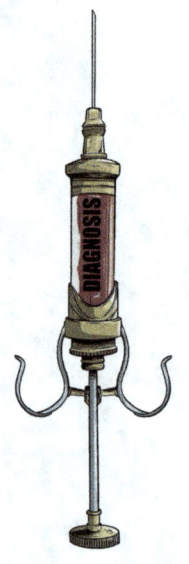

Chapter 2
The Results

I t was almost a week after the emergency room visit. I tried not to worry too much—I didn't want to add more stress to what I was already dealing with. Still, I'd had several issues since then, almost mimicking the incident from the other night. This time, though, it was just my leg—not the entire left side of my body.

I was sitting at home watching TV when my stomach began to rumble. I was hungry—actually starving. I hadn't been intentionally starving myself, but I hadn't had much of an appetite since everything happened.

I searched through the cabinets, hoping to find something to eat. Nothing piqued my interest. Finally, I decided I was going to treat myself to something delicious. I called Jack to see if he was hungry, too. He agreed to meet me.

We met at my favorite steakhouse in downtown Eastport. I ordered my favorite cut—the filet mignon, medium rare, with a side of mashed potatoes. Jack went for his usual: country-fried steak. I know they call it a steak, but I've always believed that at a steakhouse, you should get a *real* steak. Still, I didn't judge—he orders it every time.

We sat and talked for over an hour, reminiscing about our glory days in high school. Jack and I have been best friends since then. It's wild to think our friendship has lasted this long.

Back in high school, I was on the varsity football team, and Jack played baseball. He'd hoped to make it big, maybe even go pro someday. But during a game against one of our biggest rivals, he suffered a serious injury that benched him for the rest of the season. He never played the same after that. It crushed him. He kept playing through high school, but he never made it any further. It still stings for him, but he loves reliving those days.

As we were eating, Jack brought up the night

I cut my hand.

"What *really* happened?" he asked. "You were in the ER a long time for a simple cut."

I told him it was late, and the doctors wanted to keep an eye on me because I hit the side of my head when I fell. They were worried it might be a concussion. I don't think he fully believed me, but he didn't push it.

I asked if he'd be willing to take me to my appointment the next morning—for my *hand check-up*. He agreed without hesitation.

After we left the restaurant, he suddenly stopped and pointed across the street, toward the town's bookstore.

"Isn't that the doctor from the other night?"

I followed his gaze. A man was getting into a burgundy Oldsmobile, holding several books. It was Dr. Bachman. He had no cane. No limp. No sign of physical difficulty at all.

"Didn't he have a cane?" Jack asked.

"Yeah, weird," I replied. "Well, thanks for coming with me, Jack. It's been a long week."

"No problem. I'll see you tomorrow," he said, and we went our separate ways.

On the drive home, I couldn't get the image of Dr. Bachman without his cane out of my head. I know—he *did* say he didn't always need it. But would he really be walking that easily if he had a genuine issue with his leg? I shrugged it off again, telling myself it was nothing, we rode quietly the rest of the ride home.

That night at home, I was getting ready for bed. Following my usual routine, I stepped out of the shower—and suddenly, my leg gave out. It just stopped working.

I sat on the edge of the bathtub, stunned. I tried to stand, but my leg refused to cooperate. The stress began to mount as I thought about the possible news I'd be receiving tomorrow. After sitting there for a few minutes, the mobility in my leg slowly returned. I managed to get up and finish getting ready for bed.

I laid in bed for what felt like an hour before I finally drifted off to sleep. I had a dream that night well some might call it a nightmare. It was something I haven't dreamt about in ages. It was my father, and one of the last few times that I saw him.

When my dads condition started getting severe one of the last things he lost was the mobility in his hands. At that point in time he was strictly wheelchair bound. We were at the grocery story which was oddly placed on a hill. Jack had came with us, Me and Jack used to go everywhere together, we were inseparable. As we were leaving, my father was about to roll his chair down the ramp of the stores exit, he started to have spasms in both hands but then was unable to move them, and he began to roll down the ramp and at a uncontrollable speed.

Me and Jack tried to run and stop it, but I just couldn't catch up to him. A few feet at the front of the ramp was the handicap spot that my mom had been waiting for us at.

When he made it to the bottom of the ramp, he crashed terribly into the car. My mom jumped out the car and we got to him. He had a deep gash on his forehead. All three of us managed to get him back into the wheelchair. We went to the hospital immediately after. but after that day, my father never wanted to leave the house. I didn't know if he felt embarrassed or just scared because all of the mobility he once had was gone. I don't like to say i was scared but I didn't know what was gonna happen to me. Would that be my fate someday? would I be wheelchair bound? lose all of my mobilities?

The next morning, I was jolted awake by loud banging on the door. I shot out of bed to find Jack standing there.

I had almost overslept—if it hadn't been for Jack, I probably would have.

"Hurry the hell up, boy! We're gonna be late!" he shouted.

I rushed to get dressed, thankful that the Buster Memorial Hospital was only a short drive away.

In the waiting room, Dr. Bachman greeted both of us. He had his cane again, but I was too preoccupied to question it. There were more important things on my mind.

He led me into the examination room while Jack waited outside. The moment I stepped inside, it felt like my life flashed before my eyes. My heart sank.

Dr. Bachman showed me all the results from the tests I had undergone.

And that's when he gave me my diagnosis.

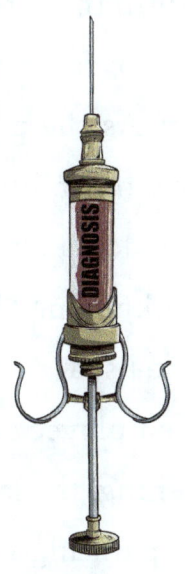

Chapter 3

Between Waking and Withering

A few weeks after the life-altering hospital visit, the familiar rhythm of my workday at the Hondel Co. factory offered a semblance of normalcy. As the production operator, the weight of responsibility was substantial, yet the routine provided a small comfort amid the encroaching unknown. The day had been long—filled with the usual demands of production schedules and employee oversight. As I left the factory that evening, the late afternoon sun cast long shadows, painting the familiar landscape in an unfamiliar light.

I settled into the driver's seat, the engine humming to life beneath my touch—a sound that had always reassured me. As I navigated the familiar route home, a sudden, inexplicable spasm seized my leg. The muscles contracted violently, causing me to wrench my hand from the steering wheel. Panic flared as the vehicle veered sharply. I fought to regain control, but the rogue signals firing through my nerves rendered my limbs unresponsive. The world outside the windshield blurred as the car careened off the road.

The sickening crunch of metal against bark and the loud shatter of glass were followed by an even more ominous sound—the groan and splintering of a large tree. The impact was brutal. Then—darkness.

I awoke to a dull throbbing in my head and the sterile scent of a hospital room. A bandage was wrapped around my forehead. Beside my bed stood Dr. Bachman—his familiar presence comforting in this disorienting reality.

"Hey, buddy. Glad you're okay," he said, his voice carrying a note of genuine concern. "You were out for a while."

"How long?" I managed to ask, my throat dry.

"About twenty-four hours," he replied. "Do

you remember what happened?"

Fragmented images flickered in my mind. "I was leaving work... my hands spasmed... I lost control... the tree... then nothing."

He stood beside the bed and explained, "As your disease progresses, symptoms like this are going to happen a lot more often. We'll have to run blood work periodically to monitor the progression over the next few months. Meanwhile, I'm going to prescribe you two medications—one to help slow the progression, though it won't cure this horrible disease, and the other for the pain. Don't forget to take them. You'll be able to leave tomorrow."

I asked him if the bloodwork was truly necessary. He affirmed that it was. I found it odd since I had already received my diagnosis—but he was a doctor; he would know better.

My gaze drifted to the sling on his arm. "What happened to your hand?" I asked.

"Fell on my way out of the shower," he sighed. "Landed on it trying to break my fall. Managed to sprain it."

"I hope it gets better," I offered.

"Thanks," he said, turning to leave. "Get some rest."

As I drifted back to sleep, a bizarre, unsettling dream took hold. In that hazy realm between consciousness and unconsciousness, I saw Dr. Bachman slipping into my room. His movements were furtive, his eyes glinting in the dim light. I tried to call out, to move, but my body felt heavy, unresponsive. He approached my bedside, and I saw the glint of a needle. He drew vials of blood—his actions swift and clinical. The dream was vivid, disturbing—yet the lingering effects of the morphine left me unsure of its reality.

The next morning, I awoke with a clearer sense of my surroundings. The insistent pangs of hunger reminded me of my prolonged unconsciousness. I reached for the hospital phone and ordered breakfast. Ten minutes later, a tray arrived—the aroma of meatloaf and mashed potatoes surprisingly appealing. Hospital food, contrary to popular belief, could occasionally hit the spot.

As I finished eating, Dr. Bachman returned, holding discharge papers. "You're free to leave whenever you're ready," he announced. "But I need you back next month for a checkup."

An hour later, I walked out of the hospital. Jack met me in the parking lot and drove me straight home. The familiarity of my house was a welcome sight. Shedding the hospital gown for the comfort of my own clothes, I began my usual bedtime ritual. Though I was still in pain, I craved the normalcy of routine.

I stepped into the shower, the shampoo stinging the cuts left by the shattered glass.

Afterward, I began brushing my teeth. While brushing, my hand suddenly spasmed and then dropped, lifeless. The spasm stopped, but I couldn't move that arm. I was tired—physically and mentally—worn down by this horrid disease. Eventually, I managed to finish and lay in bed, the weight of my situation pressing down on me.

The accident—a direct consequence of the disease's progression—was a stark and terrifying reminder of what lay ahead. The future stretched before me: uncertain, shadowed by the relentless advance of MS.

There was no escaping this reality, no miracle cure on the horizon. The only path forward was to follow Dr. Bachman's instructions—to take the medication that might offer a slight reprieve, a slowing of the inevitable decline.

I tried to quiet the storm of thoughts swirling in my mind, to find a moment of peace amid the growing anxiety. Eventually, exhaustion claimed me, and I drifted into a troubled sleep.

This time, the dream was more visceral—more terrifying. Dr. Bachman was there again, in my bedroom. I felt a crushing weight on my chest, holding me down, rendering me immobile. From outside my window came a deep, ominous creaking, like a massive tree swaying precariously in a storm. The sound grew louder, closer—and then, with a deafening crash, a massive tree slammed through the roof directly above me. I watched as Dr. Bachman moved with impossible speed, dodging the falling debris. But I was trapped, pinned beneath splintering wood and collapsing plaster. The weight was immense, suffocating.

I jolted awake, gasping for breath, my heart pounding. The terror lingered, so intense it felt real. I sat up, but my legs immediately gave out, buckling beneath me. I stumbled forward, catching myself on the edge of the bed. A wave of nausea swept over me. I made my way to the bathroom, the cool tile stark against the clammy sweat on my skin. Splashing cold water on my face, I tried to shake off the remnants of the nightmare—to fully wake from the dread still clinging to me.

The clock told me the entire day had slipped away—it was already ten o'clock at night. The need to move, to escape the house and the suffocating weight of my thoughts, became overwhelming. Reluctantly, I changed into my running clothes and headed out into the night. The cool air was a welcome sensation against my face as I began to run, pushing my body in search of a distraction, a reprieve. The rhythmic pounding of my feet on the pavement was familiar and grounding. The quiet streets of my neighborhood, draped in darkness, offered a strange comfort—a temporary shield from the harsh realities of my waking life.

The next morning, the lingering effects of my late-night run revealed themselves in the stiffness of my muscles. But mentally, the fog had lifted—if only slightly. After a simple breakfast of sausage and eggs, I began preparing for work. Even though, I was able to secure a rental car, I had felt I could no longer trust myself behind the wheel at least currently, I called Jack and asked if he could pick me up. True to form, he arrived ten minutes later.

As we drove to the factory, Jack glanced over, concern etched into his features. "You okay to be back at work so soon?" he asked.

"Yeah, I'm fine," I replied—perhaps with more conviction than I truly felt.

"Glad you weren't hurt too badly," he said quietly.

The rest of the drive passed in comfortable silence. Though Jack and I were longtime friends, I still hadn't shared everything about my diagnosis. I had only led him to believe it was all related to the cut on my hand and the wreck that followed.

When we arrived, the familiar clatter of machinery was momentarily drowned out by the applause of my employees. Their warm smiles and well wishes were genuine. This wasn't just a workplace—it was a family.

We returned to our routines, and the familiar tasks offered a small measure of solace.

Later that morning, while reviewing production reports, I held my clipboard in my left hand. Without warning, a spasm gripped me. My hand cramped violently, the muscles seizing with sharp pain. The clipboard slipped from my grasp, clattering to the floor. My fingers locked into a contorted position, throbbing with intense ache. Panic surged as the stiffness held. It lasted only seconds—but it felt like an eternity. When the pain finally eased, my hand remained frozen, paralyzed and unresponsive.

Despair washed over me. This was it—the relentless progression of the disease. Tasks I had once performed without thought were now becoming insurmountable.

I looked for Jack, my voice tight with frustration and helplessness. "Could you take me home? I'm not really feeling the best."

He nodded without a word, his expression mirroring my own dread. He drove me back, silent but present, then he returned to the factory and took over my daily duties in my absence. I went straight to bed, the weight of the day and the grim truth of my declining condition pressing down on me.

Rest offered only a brief escape. The anxiety remained—constant, oppressive, inescapable. I was deeply shaken by what had happened to my hand. It was more than a physical setback; it was a clear, painful reminder of the battle I faced—a battle I knew I could not win.

Chapter 4
Falling Quietly

The following month, the sterile scent of the hospital corridors carried a different weight—no longer just clinical, but laced with quiet dread. Beneath the surface of my forced composure stirred a nervous flutter, subtle yet insistent. Jack, ever the steady presence in the growing chaos of my life, still believed this was just a routine checkup from the wreck.

He maneuvered his truck through the sluggish afternoon traffic. Our usual rhythm of conversation was replaced by silence thick with unspoken fears. When he pulled up to the now-familiar entrance, he offered a look—part question, part comfort. I gave a quick wave and stepped alone into the fluorescent hum of the clinic.

The wait was short, no more than five minutes, yet it stretched unbearably as I mentally retraced the past week's unsettling events. When Dr. Bachman finally emerged, I noticed the difference instantly. The confident—if slightly eccentric—physician from our earlier encounters was somehow diminished. The brace on his hand was gone, but a fresh splint now wrapped his left arm, and his gait had changed—no longer favoring the right leg as before, but now limping on the left. It was a subtle but jarring inversion, enough to send a ripple of unease through me.

He approached with a syringe and vial in hand, his expression distant and oddly flat.

"I need to take some blood work," he said, his tone devoid of its usual warmth.

A flicker of irritation rose in me. "Why? Haven't you taken enough already?" The words slipped out sharper than intended—the edge of my exhaustion showing.

"Mike, like I told you at your last visit—we need to monitor the progression. I know this feels like torture, but it's the only way to know how to adjust treatment and keep the disease from progressing even more rapidly," he replied, eyes flicking away for a brief moment.

"Really?" I pressed, my skepticism obvious.

"Yes, sir," he said, a hint of defensiveness creeping into his voice.

"Okay, whatever," I sighed, too tired to argue. He inserted the needle; the sting barely registered against the churn of thoughts in my head.

As he filled the vial, I couldn't help but ask, "What happened to your arm?" My voice was casual, but suspicion threaded through it.

He offered a rushed explanation—something about slamming it in a hospital door on his way out last week. It sounded flimsy, like a hastily patched excuse. I didn't press, but the unease lodged itself deeper. The altered limp, the fresh injury, the strange detachment—it all felt... off. Dr. Bachman was becoming a puzzle with too many shifting pieces.

"You'll need to come back for another check-up within the next month and a half," he said, the words delivered mechanically, as though reciting from a script. I nodded, resignation settling over me like a worn coat. Another month. Another visit. Another needle. Another layer of pain.

As I exited the hospital, a strange craving stirred in me—not for food or sleep, but for distance. I needed space, a break from the antiseptic air and creeping dread. I asked Jack if we could take a detour downtown.

He agreed without hesitation, though I could hear the concern in his voice.

The historic district of Eastport, North Carolina, offered a modest charm—cobblestone streets, aged brick buildings, iron balconies. It whispered echoes of a quieter time, a simpler one. As we drove, I thought of running there again—the steady beat of my feet on uneven stones offering a fleeting illusion of control. A breath. A pause. A moment's escape from the ever-tightening grip of the unknown.

Jack dropped me off near the waterfront, where a gentle breeze carried the salty tang of the Eastport River. He offered to walk with me, but I told him I just needed to be alone for a little bit.

I wandered for a while, letting the familiar sights wrap around me like a warm blanket—the vibrant murals splashed across time-worn brick, the Riverwalk buzzing with a patchwork of tourists and locals, laughter mingling with the call of distant gulls. Eventually, the familiar pull of the runner's high beckoned, and I began a slow, steady jog.

For twenty glorious minutes, I felt almost like myself again. The exertion, the focused rhythm of my breath, the brief flickers of strength in my limbs—it was a welcome distraction from the quiet betrayal unfolding within my body. I approached the iconic water fountain in the heart of the square, its cascading waters glittering in the late light, hypnotic in their motion.

And then—without warning—my left leg gave out.

The ground came up fast. The impact knocked the wind from my lungs, and pain flared sharply in my knee. I tried to rise, but my leg wouldn't respond. It was dead weight, as if it no longer belonged to me. Panic bloomed in my chest—raw and icy.

A man rushed over—a kind-faced stranger with worried eyes.

"Are you alright?" he asked, already kneeling beside me, his voice steady with concern as he helped me to a nearby bench.

He introduced himself as David. He told me

he was just leaving his apartment and was in a rush to get to an important doctor's appointment, but he'd be happy to give me a ride home on the way there—just so I wouldn't risk falling again if I was alone. I thanked him, my voice tight with embarrassment, and told him I already had a ride. He gave me a reassuring nod and then hurried off.

I pulled out my phone and called Jack. He picked up on the second ring, his usual cheer immediately replaced by concern as I explained what had happened. Within minutes, his truck pulled up to the curb like clockwork.

Before heading home, Jack made an unexpected stop. He disappeared into a small medical supply store and returned moments later carrying a cane, the aluminum catching the glow of the streetlights.

"Here," he said gently. "Maybe this can help you get around a bit safer for now."

His thoughtfulness hit me harder than the fall. A balm to my frayed nerves. A reminder that even as my body faltered, I wasn't facing this alone.

But a cane. I never imagined I'd need a cane.

The ride home was quiet. Not an awkward silence, but a heavy one—filled with the unspoken truth that things were changing, and fast. The cane felt foreign in my hand, a cold metal symbol of the freedom I was rapidly losing.

Jack helped me inside, his grip firm but unobtrusive. Once alone, the weight of the day sank in with crushing clarity. Running—once my escape, my therapy—had left me broken on the pavement. The disease was no longer creeping. It was charging. And I could no longer deny where it was taking me.

In bed I laid there, staring at the ceiling for a long time before opening my laptop. I needed answers—real ones. I typed in: *How often is blood work needed for monitoring the progression of Multiple Sclerosis?*

The search results came quickly—and what I saw made my stomach churn. Blood work is typically used **only for diagnosis** or to rule out other conditions—not for monitoring the progression of MS.

I stared at the screen, my eyes narrowing. Then widening.

All those visits. All that blood. Why?

Sleep eventually came, more from exhaustion than peace. But even in dreams, the unease remained—the fall, the cane, the kind stranger, Jack's steady presence that illuminated the darkness... but only briefly.

Because deep down, I knew: The darkness was growing. And I was running out of places to hide.

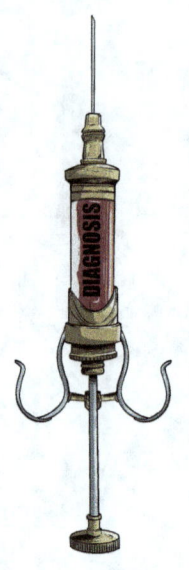

Chapter 5

The Doctor's Mask

Part One

The next day, before I arrived for my next checkup, I called ahead and managed to schedule a consultation with a Dr. Burlow at New Hanover Regional Medical Center, that would be shortly after my appointment with Dr. Bachman. I was determined to inform him of what I had discovered during my research into my alleged disease.

When Dr. Bachman entered the room, there was a stark and unsettling shift. The limp that had previously affected one of his legs had disappeared from both—yet he still wore a splint. When he asked about my cane, I explained that I still couldn't move my leg properly. His dismissive response—"That's terrible"—left me deeply unsettled, not because of what he said but how he said it. It felt ingenuine.

Curious, I asked about his cane. He claimed he had finally undergone surgery, but my suspicions grew when I noticed a syringe in his hand and he requested more blood. My frustration boiled over. I expressed my anger and told him about my research from the night before—that bloodwork was reportedly not necessary for monitoring the disease. His repeated, robotic reply—"It's just our hospital's procedure"—only intensified my irritation.

Pushed to my limit, I rose with my cane and declared my intention to stop monitoring the disease and to stop seeing the "good ole doctor." I told him I would seek a second opinion. As I reached the threshold of the door, Dr. Bachman gripped my shoulder firmly to stop me from leaving. His immediate and vehement objection—"No, you can't do that"—only strengthened my resolve.

With a final, defiant "Screw you, doctor," I yanked my arm from his grasp and left the examination room—determined and ready to see Dr. Burlow, who I hoped would finally offer clarity and honesty about my condition.

The encounter left me shaken and deeply distrustful. His evasive answers, the inconsistencies in his physical ailments, and the unexplained, persistent need for blood raised serious red flags. Seeking a second opinion was no longer just about confirming or denying the Multiple Sclerosis diagnosis—it had become a quest for the truth.

Jack agreed without hesitation to drive me to the hospital in Wilmington not to far from Eastport for my next appointment. On the ride there, anxiety mingled with anticipation.

As I waited for my consultation, Jack remained in the waiting room while I was called back to meet Dr. Burlow. That was when I finally revealed everything that had happened over the past few months with this so-called "diagnosis." He was shocked and stunned by what I told him.

I was then called into the examination room. When I entered, the doctor was already there.

Dr. Burlow's direct but reassuring manner was immediately comforting. I explained that Dr. Bachman at Buster Memorial Hospital had diagnosed me with Multiple Sclerosis. Aware of the seriousness of such a diagnosis, Dr. Burlow explained that many tests were necessary to confirm the presence of specific markers—but blood work was not typically needed to monitor the disease's progression.

I was desperate for clarity amidst the growing confusion and dread. He offered to run a few tests. I was reluctant—after all, I had already been fooled once. Did I really want to risk it again? But it seemed like the only way to possibly get to the truth. He also had me sign a release to get the records back from the Buster Memorial Hospital. The hour-long wait for the results felt endless.

When Dr. Burlow returned, his news was both shocking and relieving: He said the test seemed to show no abnormalities. but came next left me speechless. He said that he received the records back, and that was never an official diagnosis of Multiple Sclerosis. In the notes, it only said "possible Hemiplegic migraine from possible head trauma from sport related injuries". He suggested that Dr. Bachman had likely misinterpreted the initial results. While the relief was immense. I asked him how exactly could a doctor misinterpret such a serious diagnosis like such. Dr. Burlow just couldn't seem to come up with an answer.

I asked him what about all the symptoms that I have been experiencing, and To my astonishment, Dr. Burlow proposed a psychological explanation: my symptoms might have been a psychosomatic reaction, triggered by the trauma and fear of the initial diagnosis. Encouraged to try moving, I stood up—wobbly at first—but then walked on my own. A rush of disbelief and emotion flooded through me.

When I returned to the waiting room, Jack looked stunned as I told him I no longer needed the cane. We left for home in silence, the day's events swirling in my mind, leaving a trail of confusion and unease.

He drove me home and told me he would do a little digging himself. He mentioned he knew a few nurses who worked at the Hospital and would ask around. He even suggested going to meet the "ole doctor" himself. I told him not to do anything of the sort—that I would get to the bottom of everything myself. This was my battle to fight. He assured me he wouldn't, but he didn't sound entirely convincing.

Not long after Jack left, I sat in bed, unable to even think about sleep and driven by a restless need for answers, I decided I was going to return to the Hospital and confront the doctor like Jack wanted to do. I called Jack a few times, but it rang and rang with no answer. I didn't think it was the best idea to go alone, but I wanted answers, and I wanted them immediately. When I got to the hospital the parking lot was nearly empty. The night air was cool and still. The only sounds were the faint rustle of leaves and the distant hum of traffic. I roamed the lot for almost twenty minutes until I finally found Dr. Bachman's burgundy Oldsmobile.

That's when I saw his figure exiting the dim hospital entrance—his gait instantly recognizable. My pulse quickened.

As Dr. Bachman approached, it was almost as if he knew I was already out there waiting. Before I could say a word, he rushed at me, holding a syringe. I moved fast, trying to block his sudden attack, adrenaline surging. I grabbed his shoulder.

He then swung the needle quickly, jabbing me in the side of the neck. His eyes were widened expressions somewhere between fury and panic. The world tipped violently. The asphalt rushed up to meet me.

Darkness closed in, but just before everything faded, I hear done final, chilling sound: the metallic click of a car trunk opening—and then closing.

I rustled around for a few seconds; my vision began to blur and then suddenly the darkness overtook me.

Chapter 6

The Doctor's Mask

Part Two

J ack was shocked by what Mike had revealed to him. It seemed utterly unbeliev-
able—what kind of doctor could do that to a
patient? He had heard stories about such things
happening, but never imagined it could happen
to his best friend. Still reeling, Jack made his
way home.

That night, while lying in bed, Jack called a
few nurses he knew from high school. Each had
something kind to say about Dr. Bachman; not a
single bad comment was made. When he asked
about the doctor's physical condition, they all
told the same story: Dr. Bachman had been in a
terrible accident when he was younger and was
still dealing with its lingering effects. Despite
these reassurances, Jack resolved to confront
the doctor directly.

Late that night, Jack left his house and headed to the hospital, hoping Dr. Bachman was
still there. At the front desk, he spun a story

about needing to see the doctor due to terrible side effects from some medication he'd been prescribed. The receptionist told him he would need to make an appointment unless it was an emergency, in which case he'd have to go to the Emergency Room. She added that, in any case, the doctor had just left for the night a few minutes earlier.

Determined, Jack decided to try catching the doctor in the parking lot before he could leave. He searched the area but couldn't find him. As Jack was walking past his own car, Dr. Bachman drove by. Jack quickly jumped into his car and began to follow him.

After five minutes on the road, Dr. Bachman stopped at a small, run-down gas station. Jack made sure not to park within the doctor's line of sight. He then watched as Dr. Bachman got out of his car—remarkably, without using a cane. At the corner of the gas station sat a police car. Jack observed as Dr. Bachman approached the officer and handed over an envelope. Jack sat there, his mind racing with questions about what might be inside it. After the exchange, Dr. Bachman returned to his car and drove away, with Jack continuing to follow.

About ten minutes later, Dr. Bachman arrived at a luxurious home in one of the city's most exclusive neighborhoods. Jack watched as the doctor entered the house. Jack hesitated, debating what to do next, but ultimately decided he would still confront him. He exited his car and approached the front door.

Jack stood at the door, summoning the courage to knock. As he raised his fist, the door suddenly swung open.

"Good evening, Jack. Did you really think I wouldn't notice you tailing me all the way home?" the doctor asked.

Jack was stunned—he had been sure he'd

been discreet. Speechless, he stood frozen in the doorway. The doctor then invited Jack inside for a "little conversation," making it clear that if he didn't comply, he would call his friend from the police force. Jack entered, determined to get answers to his questions.

Chapter 7

An Unsuccessful Operation

I was not always an evil doctor. An unsuccessful attempt to save a life brought me to the position I am in now. I was once a decorated physician—respected, trusted. Now, I'm seen as a spawn of Satan. One heartbroken gypsy mother brought the darkness that now defines me into this world. I can't say I blame her. But I also don't believe it was right. As doctors, we are not always able to save everyone—though we wish we could.

I had been a doctor for 20 years, and the first life I failed to save became the worst day of my life. His name was Kamill Lovell. He was only 16.

Kamill's family was well known in town—but not for good reasons. They were the last openly known gypsy family in the area. Rumors swirled that his mother was a gypsy witch, though nothing was ever proven.

Kamill was a gifted young man. An athletic, bright student—a varsity football player for Eastport High School and also the class valedictorian. The night it all ended was the night of the final football game. Everything was on the line. A win would have secured him a full scholarship to the University of Wilmington, North Carolina.

It ended in a single, brutal moment.

Kamill was sprinting down the field, wide open. The ball soared across the field, landing smoothly in his hands. As he crossed into the end zone, the adrenaline-fueled momentum of a defensive player carried him forward. He tried to stop himself, but he couldn't. His helmet slammed into Kamill's just after the touchdown. Kamill's helmet flew off, and his head hit the ground—hard.

It was a terrifying sight. Kamill's father later said it was the hardest he had ever seen someone get hit.

The defensive player got back on his feet, but Kamill lay motionless. The coach ran to him and found him unresponsive. He signaled for the medics. Kamill's parents ran down from the stands. His mother was screaming. His father held him close. Medics carefully slid Kamill onto the stretcher and rushed him to the waiting ambulance.

It was 9:00 p.m. when Kamill arrived at the emergency room. The high school was 20 minutes away. It was a miracle he made it alive. The full extent of his injuries became clear only after the brain scan. He was still unconscious when he arrived. His mother clung to her husband, eyes full of panic.

We immediately took Kamill for a CT scan.

As he lay in the hospital bed, his parents at his side, my surgical team and I rushed into the room. I quickly informed them: Kamill had a severe brain bleed and needed emergency surgery.

His mother begged me to save her baby boy.

I made a critical mistake that day—the kind a doctor should never make.

I told her I would save him.

We're trained to say, *"I will do my best,"* or *"I will do everything I can."* But I said *I would.* I believed it. I had done this surgery a hundred times. I didn't doubt myself. Not until that night.

We rushed Kamill into the operating room.

I examined the CT scan again. A thin red line cut across the image—a fresh bleed. Kamill, that brilliant and athletic sixteen-year-old, lay on the table. His brain, normally a beautiful landscape of intricate folds, now bore a vivid red smear. I'd seen many bleeds in my career, but it never got easier—especially not with someone so young. Every case like this reminded me how quickly life could unravel.

The OR was filled with a tense silence, broken only by the rhythmic beeping of the heart monitor. My team worked with precise urgency. Elena, my nurse of many years, handed me instruments with practiced ease. The soft hum of the ventilator was the only other sound beneath my steady voice giving instructions.

I began the craniotomy. The high-speed drill always felt too powerful in such a fragile space. Peeling back the layers—bone, dura, and arachnoid—was like uncovering a living map. The acrid scent of cauterized tissue filled the room; a familiar, metallic reminder of the life I'd chosen.

Then, the brain.

Its normally creamy, smooth surface was swollen and distorted near the hemorrhage. I leaned into the microscope, carefully navigating the maze of neural tissue. My instruments were an extension of my hands—tiny tools dancing delicately across the most sensitive part of the human body.

And still... I failed. That was when I found it—a tiny, stubborn vessel still leaking blood.

With a steady hand, I attempted to clip it, my fingers aching from the effort of absolute stillness. The first clip slipped. A ripple of panic, almost imperceptible, passed through the room. I adjusted and tried again. This time, it held. A collective, unspoken sigh of relief filled the air.

For a moment, hope flared.

The bleeding slowed... then stopped. I straightened slightly, a bead of sweat trickling down my temple. Carefully, I began the meticulous process of rinsing the area, preparing to close.

Then the monitor screamed.

Kamill's blood pressure plummeted. Elena's voice, usually calm, turned sharp with urgency ."Dr. Bachman, he's crashing!"

My eyes snapped from the microscope to the monitors. The steady beeping had transformed into a frantic, flatline wail. The bleed I thought I had controlled had erupted again—larger, more violent. The entire surgical field became a churning, dark pool, obscuring everything beneath.

A cold dread seeped into my bones—that familiar, unwelcome feeling.

I worked frantically, searching for the new source. But it was like trying to plug a dam with a single finger. The blood surged, unstoppable. I could feel Kamill's life slipping away beneath my hands—a cruel irony after all our efforts.

"We're losing him!" Elena's voice cracked, filled with desperation.

I kept fighting, my movements a blur, a desperate, futile dance. The brain throbbed beneath my tools—not just a surgical field anymore, but a living organ collapsing under trauma. I knew then, with a gut-wrenching certainty: it was over.

The monitors screamed their final, mournful song.Flatline.

I straightened slowly. My shoulders sagged. The sterile air of the operating room felt heavy, suffocating. The silence that followed the final beep was deafening.

I looked down at the still, innocent face of the boy—gone. And the weight of my failure crushed me. I had fought. I had tried. But this time, the bleed had won.

And this... was just the beginning of my inevitable downfall.

I removed my blood-soaked surgical garments and tossed them into the biohazard waste bin. Then I left the operating room, my chest tight, my heart pounding.

This was the first time in my career that I had lost someone and failing to save someone so young made the pain even worse.

As I stepped into the room where Kamill's

parents waited, I could feel my pulse quicken. They looked up at me—and before I could even speak, his mother collapsed. She crumpled to the floor, sobbing. Kamill's father dropped down beside her, holding her in his arms.

I stood there, silent.

I could only imagine their pain. I had never experienced anything like it myself. But I knew the depth of that hurt. I could feel it all around me. And I knew nothing I said could ever make it right.

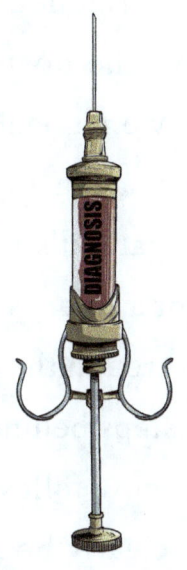

Chapter 8

A Gypsy's Curse

A week after the unsuccessful operation, I was leaving work one night. As I exited the double doors of the hospital, I noticed a figure sitting quietly on a bench just outside. I walked past without saying anything, assuming it was just another patient's family member or someone waiting for a ride.

But as I moved through the parking lot, I became aware of footsteps behind me. The figure had stood and was now following—keeping a little distance, but clearly headed in the same direction. I didn't think much of it at first and continued toward my car. But when I reached it and turned around, the figure was still following.

I decided to confront them.

"Is there something I can help you with?" I asked, my voice cautious but stern.

The figure kept walking toward me. As the dim lights of the lot revealed more of their features, my stomach turned.

"Mrs. Lovell?"

It was Kamill's mother.

She stepped directly in front of me. In one fluid motion, she pulled out a small cloth bag that looked ancient—covered in strange markings I didn't recognize. She untied the string and poured a grayish substance into her palm. Before I could react, she blew the dust into my face.

Instantly, I couldn't breathe. My chest tightened, my blood felt as if it were boiling inside me. An unbearable heat surged through my limbs. My body locked up, and a searing paralysis overtook me. I collapsed.

Mrs. Lovell stood over me, her face unreadable. Then she shouted words that would haunt me forever:"**Tu ka poćines, vaś mire ćhavenqe dukh.**" Unsure of what it meant, It still sent a sharp shiver down my spine.

My vision blurred. My eyes grew heavy. And then—darkness. I fell into a deep, unnatural sleep.

I awoke the next morning in my own bed, drenched in sweat. I had almost no memory of the night before—just a vague image of Mrs. Lovell and those strange, burning words echoing in my head.

As the months passed, I began to feel… changed. Weaker. Not just physically, but mentally. My thoughts turned darker. I found myself short-tempered, quick to anger, even with those I trusted. There were days I lashed out at the nurses. Most believed I was still grieving the loss of Kamill. But I knew something deeper was unraveling inside me.

One day at work, my leg gave out without warning. It buckled under me, leaving me clutching the wall for support. I told myself it was age—or stress—but I knew better. Her words had never left me. They echoed more loudly with each passing day.

That evening, I drove straight to the Lovells' shop.

As I approached the door, Mrs. Lovell opened it—almost as if she had been expecting me.

Without a word, she turned and walked to the back. I followed. We entered a room unlike any I'd ever seen—a shrine to Kamill.

Hundreds of photos lined the walls, all of Kamill. In the center of the room stood a small altar. On it sat an urn, a burning candle, and the same small sack she had once used on me.

She gestured for me to sit.

I did.

Then, without hesitation, she opened Kamill's urn. Using her hand, she scooped out a small amount of his ashes and poured them into the sack.

I watched in shock, speechless. My breath caught in my throat. I didn't know what to say—what to do. Something ancient and unknowable filled the room, and I could feel its weight pressing down on my chest.

I was no longer sure what I believed. But one thing was certain.

This wasn't grief.

This was something much, much older.

And it had chosen me.

She sat across from me, her eyes locking onto mine with an unnerving intensity, as if she were peering straight into the deepest recesses of my soul. Without breaking her gaze, she spoke in a low, chilling voice.

"I know why you're here, Dr. Bachman," she said, her words carrying a strange weight. "You want me to diagnose you. But I've already done that. I've put a curse on you. That's why you've been feeling... *weak*."

I froze. My heart pounded in my chest, a mixture of shock and growing fury bubbling up inside me.

"Why? Why would you do that?" My voice trembled despite my efforts to remain composed.

She slammed her palm onto the table, her fury mirroring mine.

"You're a doctor, Dr. Bachman. You're supposed to save lives. But you didn't save my boy! My sweet Kamill—he had everything to live for!" Her voice cracked, but there was no softness in it. Only raw, unbridled grief.

In that moment, something inside me snapped. I shot to my feet, shouting, "I did everything I could! Your son was gone the moment he hit his head. There was nothing more I could do!" The words felt like a burning release, but they didn't even seem to reach her.

She stood, her face twisted with rage.

"I don't think you did your best!" she screamed,

each word cutting like a knife. "And you'd better watch your tone when you speak of my boy!" Her voice dropped, dangerously calm, before she leaned in closer, her words cold and venomous.

"If you want this curse lifted, you'll listen—and heed my words carefully."

She sat back down, her eyes narrowing as she studied me like a predator assessing its prey. "My boy was strong—mentally, physically. You took that away from him the moment you let him die on that table. Now, I've made you weak. Your body will deteriorate—slowly at first, then faster—until you are completely paralyzed. Mind, body, soul. There is no cure for this. But... there is something you can do to temporarily recover."

I could feel the rage building inside me, but I fought to keep it contained. I needed answers. My voice was strained, barely able to hold it together.

"What do I do? Please, Mrs. Lovell. Help me."

She leaned forward, her breath close enough for me to feel it against my skin.

"You want to be strong again? You'll need to transfer blood... but not just from anyone. It has to be from someone as strong as my boy. And you'd better make sure they believe there's something wrong with them—make them believe, just like you made us believe there was hope for our boy."

I stared at her, dumbfounded.

"Transfer blood?" I asked, my voice barely a whisper.

She smirked, a cruel twist to her lips.

"You're a doctor, Dr. Bachman. I'm sure you know all about transfusions. You must do the same... but to yourself."

A cold shiver ran down my spine as I processed her words. It sounded insane. Impossible.

"And how the hell am I supposed to do that?"

She didn't answer directly. Instead, she reached into a small, weathered pouch at her side and pulled out a handful of Kamill's ashes. She blew them gently into the air, and the fine dust settled over my face.

Instantly, I was hit with a rush of pain—agonizing, blinding—like a flashback to the torment I'd felt in the parking lot the night before.

My breath hitched. I could feel my body trembling, as though the curse she'd placed on me was now creeping deeper into my bones.

"Good luck, Dr. Bachman," she whispered softly, her voice laced with something dark, something final. As I was leaving her shop, she handed me a cane stating "You might need this doctor" then releasing a sinister giggle. Almost a month after the two interactions with Mrs. Lovell is when I started experiencing the symptoms of this alleged curse. I was in disbelief of what was happening to me that I ran several test on myself. I tested everything I could thing of and found nothing. All the symptoms closely resembled symptoms of Multiple Sclerosis. I then quickly tried to devise some plan to cure myself even if temporarily, like the gypsy said. That's when Mr. Henson walked through my doors, and I knew just what I had to do, and when I started. I felt myself getting more and more evil, and oddly enough. Maybe I liked it.

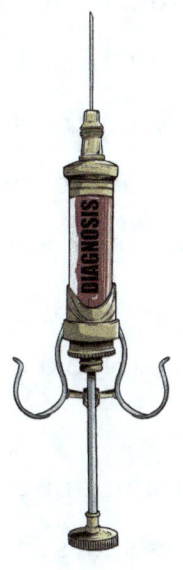

Chapter 9

No One Believes Me

Awakening to the chill of a dirt-floored basement, I found myself bound to a hospital gurney beneath the dim glow of a single bulb. Pipes snaked across the ceiling, their rhythmic dripping echoing the unease growing inside me. I looked over and saw an IV was injected into my arm. Panic began to rise, fear slowly overtaking me. I looked around the room, heart pounding.

Then, Dr. Bachman appeared, descending the creaking wooden stairs in his white coat. In one hand, he held a cane—but he wasn't using it to walk, merely carrying it like an ornament of authority or threat.

I feigned sleep, bracing myself for the unknown.

But I couldn't hold it in—I screamed helplessly.

He walked over and struck me with the tip of his cane. His words were chilling—not that he *wanted* to do this, but that he *had* to.

The truth unraveled like a nightmare: I did **not** have Multiple Sclerosis. In a horrifying confession, Dr. Bachman revealed the real cause of my suffering—a curse placed upon *him* by a gypsy witch mourning the loss of her son, who had died on his operating table. His desperate plan? To replace his failing blood with mine, clinging to the twisted promise of temporary relief offered by the witch. He explained, with unnerving calm, that he would slowly extract some of my blood—while also removing some of his own—then replace his loss with mine.

My blood was his grotesque salvation—a temporary lifeline to stave off the paralysis consuming him. But it came at a price: *my life*. After I died, he'd simply find someone else.

My pleas for reason were met with a chilling smile and a casual declaration of his intent to kill me—slowly.

Suddenly, the shrill ring of a phone echoed through the walls. He reached into his coat with urgency. Upon seeing who was calling, his expression changed. Without a word, he pulled a syringe from his pocket. I screamed, begged him to leave me alone—but before I could resist, he injected me with something cold and numbing.

Darkness swallowed me whole.

When I awoke, disbelief still clouded my mind. My screams were futile, swallowed by the stone basement walls—grim reminders of how deliberate and calculated his cruelty truly was. I was trapped. Not just physically, but in the unbearable reality of my impending doom.

Still bound to the gurney in the cold, damp basement, I realized something—the restraints on my arms weren't completely secure. The weathered leather straps, felt almost ancient like the gurney has sat in here for decades. Raw panic surged through me as I thrashed, testing every inch of slack. My cries bounced off the padded walls, each one a desperate cry for deliverance.

Then, a wild, reckless plan sparked in my mind: *What if I could tip the gurney?* Maybe the impact would loosen the restraints. I writhed and strained with all the strength I had left. Each jerk it felt like finally the straps were loosing when suddenly—with a thunderous crash—the metal frame toppled to the concrete floor.

Everything went black.

When I came to, I could feel that the thrashing and the fall had worked—just enough. I wriggled and pulled until, after what felt like forever, my arms were free. Working feverishly, I removed the restraints from my legs and scrambled to my feet.

Before I could climb the stairs, I scanned the

concrete hell for something—*anything*—that could aid my escape. That's when I saw it. A black body bag lying on the floor.

My breath caught as I stepped toward it, every movement slow, hesitant. I bent down and unzipped the bag, my hands trembling.

What I saw inside shattered me.

It was Jack—my closest friend. Lifeless. Cold. Gone. I had told him not to confront the doctor, why didn't he listen?

Tears streamed down my face. Grief and rage twisted inside me, collapsing into one unbearable truth: I had to get out of here. Not just for me.

For Jack.

When I made it to the top of the stairs, I found a solid metal door sealing me inside. Despair crashed over me as I slumped against the cold steel, tears streaming down my face. Then, there was a spark of hope. I had an idea—maybe not the best idea, but at this point, anything was better than nothing. Maybe I could use all of my weight, and the enormous weight of the gurney to rip the door from its hinges, I knew it was a crazy idea, but I had to try.

With all of my strength, I dragged the heavy gurney to the top of the stairs, secured one end of a rope that I had found lying on a dusty shelf to it and the other to the door handle. With a final surge of adrenaline, I hurled both of us down the stairs. The rope pulled tight. The door shrieked, groaned yet it rip off like I had hoped. but It did feel like it would eventually come away from its hinges.

I was sore and in immense pain, but I could not give up yet. I again, and again dragged the gurney to the top of the stairs. After the forth attempt, and the hinges getting looser and looser with each try, finally the door ripped from its hinges, and relief surged threw my body.

On the other side of that door was freedom. But after all this? Why had I escaped so easily? I wondered if this was part of his plan. Was he naïve enough to think I'd remain trapped forever? Or maybe he just thought he'd kill me before I ever got the chance to try.

Did it really matter now? I was free.

I emerged into the night, stumbling through the woods, disoriented and alone. Driven by instinct, I ran—through the quiet darkness that seemed to stretch for miles. The rhythm of my footsteps reminded me of my years playing football, and somehow, that memory kept me going.

Eventually, I reached a road. A sign read: *Eastport - 7 Miles*—a fragile hope flickering in the dark.

Then—headlights.

Terror spiked through me as I recognized Dr. Bachman's car. I dove into the woods, heart hammering, praying he hadn't seen me. By some miracle, he passed without stopping.

Eventually, I reached a gas station and encountered a stranger. I tried to explain what had happened to me, but to my despair, he didn't seem to care. Still, he pointed me toward the nearest police station.

It was a long walk, but relief surged through me as I finally stepped inside, ready to report my kidnapping—unaware that the disbelief and torment had only just begun.

I sat in the interview room, finally safe from the twisted doctor, and began recounting my story. But it felt as if the officer was reluctant to believe me. Exhausted and shaken, I struggled to find the right words.

He said I sounded just like some "old loon" from the Eastport Sanitarium who claimed to have seen an evil puppet with a zipper for a mouth slaughter residents at a nursing home that later exploded.

Desperate to prove my sanity, I offered to take him to where I was being held captive in the woods. Before we left, the officer made a quick phone call—I had no idea why or to whom what could be more important then my being kidnapped by some psychotic doctor?

We drove back to the forest I had escaped from. Once there, he insisted I stay in the cruiser while he searched for the basement.

Ten minutes passed. When he returned, he slid back into the driver's seat and calmly said, "There's nothing there—just a bunch of trees."

I swore I was telling the truth, begged to lead him there myself, repeated every detail again—but he disregarded every word. Without another glance, he drove us back to the station.

On the way, I saw Dr. Bachman driving past us in the opposite direction. I screamed, pleaded with the officer to turn around and chase him. But again, he ignored me.

At the station, a cell replaced the basement as my new prison.

"I'm telling the truth! Please, listen to me!" I shouted.

He just laughed. "Maybe I *should* call Eastport Sanitarium," he said.

Panic overtook me. I slammed my head against the bars—a futile protest.

Hours later, paramedics arrived. Officer Sheldon opened the cell, and they descended on me, forcefully strapping me to a gurney.

I fought, screamed, begged. But a needle silenced everything.

As the darkness pulled me under, I heard Officer Sheldon mutter,

"Dr. Bachman sends his regards."

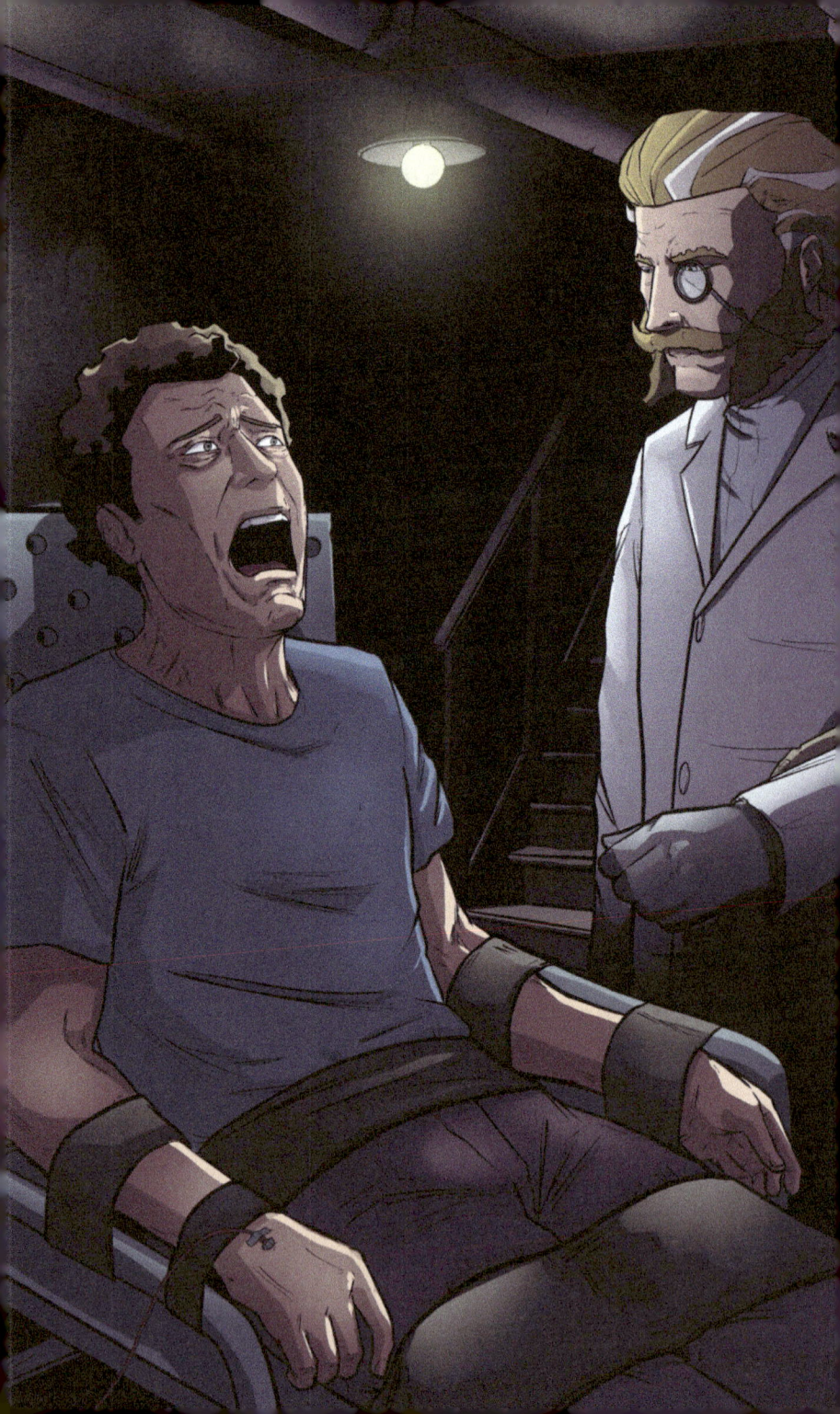

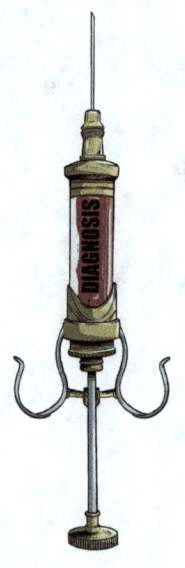

Chapter 10
The Memoir

"I've been trapped at the Eastport Sanitarium for a week now. A week since I escaped the Doctor. I'm still not sure what was real and what wasn't. They keep telling me none of it happened—but between the meds and the endless sessions with the psychiatrist, I sometimes wonder if any of it *was* real.

If it wasn't, the past few months have felt like a lifetime. The Doctor, the diagnosis, the cellar, the outrageous story of the gypsy—it was all so vivid. I *know* it was real. But here, I occasionally question my sanity. It's hard not to.

The medication puts us into a trance, but I guess that's what they want. They want you to forget everything.

But I won't.

I *refuse* to forget—not if I'm ever going to get out of this place.

I will never forget Jack—my best friend, taken from me. That was real. Dr. Bachman took everything from me. And I will do everything I can to get it back.

That's why I sit here writing this memoir—to remember. So I'll always have something to look back on, to remind myself of everything I've endured... just in case I start to forget.

There's one thing branded into my mind, echoing in my skull:

The words Officer Sheldon spoke before I was tranquilized and rolled away on that gurney—

"Dr. Bachman sends his regards."

How was Officer Sheldon involved? Was it just coincidence that he was the one to question me? What luck—for Dr. Bachman. His hostage escapes, only to walk straight into his partner's arms?

It makes me wonder—who else is working for him? The nurses here... are they part of his twisted plan? What about Dr. Harold? Is he in on it too?

I don't know.

I *wish* I knew. I wish I had all the answers.

But the truth is—I don't trust anyone any-more.

How could I? I've already been betrayed by two people I was supposed to trust: a doctor and a cop. You don't expect to walk into a hospital seeking help and get purposefully misdiagnosed. You don't expect to run into a police station after being kidnapped and be told you're a lunatic.

If I ever get out of here—*when* I get out of here—I don't know how I'll trust again.

Maybe I will. Maybe I'll learn. But I know this: I'll never let my guard down again.

And Dr. Bachman...

He won't get away with what he's done.

I'll make sure of it."

The End

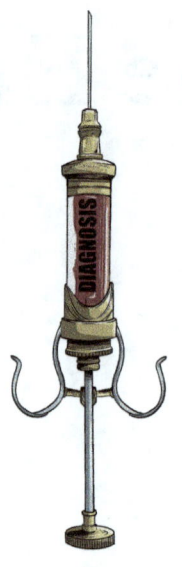

Chapter 11

After Chapter

Mike, sitting on the bed in his new hell, abruptly stopped writing in his journal when the door to his room began to open. He quickly shoved the journal and pen under his pillow just as Dr. Harold entered.

"Hey Mike," Dr. Harold said with his usual forced cheer. "Would you like to join the group today?"

Mike nodded and stood up from the bed, following Dr. Harold as he led the way toward the rec room, where the group session was being held.

As they entered, Mike scanned the room, observing the other patients. Before everything that had happened, he probably would have dismissed the entire group as a bunch of loons. But now... he wasn't so sure. Maybe he was just like them. Maybe they were all sane, in their own way.

Well—everyone except Mary.

Mary sat in the far corner of the rec room all day, whispering to someone she claimed was her boyfriend—Jesus. Sadly, the only open seat in the circle was right next to her.

At that moment, Mike regretted leaving his room with Dr. Harold.

He noticed two empty seats in the circle and carefully chose the one two spots away from Mary, trying not to look too obvious. Still, his eyes drifted to her. Her hand hovered midair, as if she were holding someone else's. She smiled faintly, humming a soft melody.

As always, Dr. Harold began the session with the same question: "How's everyone feeling today?"

The group responded with a familiar mix of groans, mumbles, or silence.

before Dr. Harold could get another word out the orderlies came slamming through the door of the rec room forcefully dragging a man into the rec room. Mike's eyes widened as he took in the sight of him—a man who looked strangely familiar. He swore he knew him, but no matter how hard he tried, the memory remained just out of reach.

"Mike, Mike!" Dr. Harold called, snapping him out of his trance. Mike blinked, still fixated on the man.

"Sorry, I just swear I know him," Mike muttered, his voice trailing off as he tried to piece together the connection.

"That's just something that comes along with your mental illness," Dr. Harold replied, irritation clear in his voice.

Mike snapped, his frustration bubbling over. "I'm not fucking crazy! Stop calling me that! I shouldn't even fucking be here!"

He stood up, pointing at the doctor in anger, his words laced with a raw desperation. Before he could even calm down, the orderlies were on him. They yanked him from behind, dragging him back to his room as the psychiatrist watched passively.

In his bed, Mike stared at the ceiling, his mind racing. He was going to remember who that man was, no matter what. Hours passed in silence, the thoughts spinning around in circles, but the answer still eluded him. Tired and drained, he finally closed his eyes, hoping that sleep might bring clarity.

When he awoke, he felt a little more rested but no less trapped. The same hellish environment. The same locked doors. Yet something had shifted in his mind.

He remembered now.

The man's name was David. He had helped Mike once—back when Mike had fallen while walking downtown. Mike couldn't move his leg, but David had come to his aid, helping him to his feet and onto a bench. But why was he here, in this dreadful place? Why was David, of all people, stuck in this nightmare?

Mike tried to recall more, but his mind was still fuzzy. He couldn't let himself assume that David was crazy just because he was here. No, he wouldn't do that. He wouldn't make the same mistake people had made with him. But something didn't sit right. This was too much of a coincidence. Mike was going to find out the truth, and he wasn't going to stop until he did.

The next morning, Mike sat in his usual seat for group therapy. He glanced over at David, who was being led to a chair by an orderly. The man looked shaken, confused, like a deer caught in headlights.

"Good morning, David," Dr. Harold greeted him, his tone clinical. "I know you're confused right now, but would you like to introduce yourself to the group?"

David shook his head, his eyes filled with

fear and uncertainty.

"That's completely okay. Maybe next time," Dr. Harold said, his voice dismissive.

"Good morning, group," Dr. Harold continued. "Did everyone sleep okay last night?"

The group, minus David and Mike, all shook their heads. The doctor's gaze shifted to Mike. "I noticed you didn't shake your head. Any reason why, Mike?"

Mike's voice was laced with bitterness. "I would give you my answer, but I don't want to get dragged away like yesterday."

Dr. Harold leaned back, crossing his arms. "As long as you stay calm, no reason you would be, Mike."

Mike slouched in his chair, crossing his arms in frustration. "I shouldn't even fucking be here."

He half-listened as the group session droned on, the words barely registering as his mind kept drifting back to David. Something was off about the whole situation, and he had to get to the bottom of it.

Later, Mike walked into the rec room and spotted David alone in the corner by the checkerboard. He was sitting in silence, his head down, eyes distant. Mike hesitated for a moment before slowly walking over and sitting across from him. Mike noticed on his head to marks, that looked as if he had gone through electro shock therapy.

"Hey, you're David, right, what happened to your head, did they use shock therapy on you?" Mike asked.

David didn't respond, but his eyes flicked up at Mike, a hint of confusion in them.

"I don't know if you remember me, but I know you... well, sort of," Mike continued, trying to sound reassuring. "I was walking downtown Eastport, and I fell—landed straight on my face. You helped me up. You helped me to a bench. I really appreciated it."

David's expression softened slightly, but he still didn't speak. There was a sense of fear in his eyes, like he wasn't sure who Mike was or what to make of him.

"Do you remember me? Or how you ended up here?" Mike asked, his voice gentle but insistent.

David turned his gaze toward him but didn't say anything. His eyes were hollow, distant.

"No," David finally muttered. "I just woke up in an ambulance, and then they were dragging me in here."

Mike's heart sank. He couldn't believe what he was hearing.

"I'm sorry, David," Mike said, his voice full of empathy. "I shouldn't even be here. They made me seem crazy, but I'm not. My doctor lied about my medical issues, was conducting some bizarre experiment on himself with the blood tests he took from me. He kidnapped me to keep his experiment going. I managed to escape, but I ended up here, and they're telling me it's all in my head. But it's not."

David looked at him with a mix of disbelief and fear. "What was his name?" he asked, his voice shaky.

Mike swallowed hard. "Dr. Bachman."

The mention of the name seemed to send David into a frenzy. His face contorted in terror, his body trembling as he stood up abruptly.

"Stop! Don't say that name! Don't say his name!" David screamed, his eyes wide with panic.

Before Mike could react, the orderlies rushed in, grabbing David and dragging him out of the room. Dr. Harold was quick to follow, injecting something into David's neck as he struggled against them.

Mike sat in his bed later that evening, the events of the day replaying in his mind. The food flap crashed open, and a tray of slop was slid through, but Mike barely noticed. He was too lost in thought, too consumed by the burning question of what had really happened to David.

The name Dr. Bachman had driven him to madness. Mike couldn't shake the feeling that there was a connection—something that tied him, David, and Dr. Bachman together. He wasn't crazy, and neither was David. The truth was out there, hidden somewhere in the fog of their memories.

Mike had to help David remember. That was the only way to prove he wasn't losing his mind. There was no way this was just a coincidence. There had to be more to it than that.

As the night dragged on, Mike steeled himself for what was to come. He wasn't giving up.

Not now. Not ever. He was going to find out the truth, even if it killed him.

While sitting in the rec room a few days after the second incident with David being dragged away, Dr. Harold walked up to Mike, and began to question him.

"Mike, why is it that after speaking with you, David had yet another outburst?"

Mike unsure of what to say, and not wanting to be dragged away by the Doctor and his goons, shrugged the question off and said "I have no idea"

Dr. Harold looked at mike not convinced with the answer Mike had given him.

"Did you mention that supposed Dr. Bachman to him maybe"

Mike shocked by Dr. Harold knowing that. "No, I didn't".

Dr. Harold calm but frustrated with Mikes answer. "I know you are lying Mike, David told us. David is not mentally well, and I don't want you to be putting crazy stories in his head, because if you keep at it, I will have to treat you the same way we treat everyone else with the same mental condition that David is going through".

Mike questioning Dr. Harold "electroshock therapy? I don't believe that is even legal here anymore, it be a shame if the state found out what you are doing here Dr. Harold".

Dr. Harold giggles "The state is very aware with what we are doing, who do you think is funding our program. I suggest you heed my warning, Mike"

Dr. Harold then stands up but before walking away says "Groups about to began, I suggest you come join us" He then walks toward the middle of the room where group is held.

Mike, stunned by the conversation, stands up from his chair. He began to wonder further, was Dr. Harold connected to Dr. Bachman? So

many thoughts ran through his head.

Mike walked over and sat down with the group. He looked at each chair and around the room, searching for David but he was no where in sight.

Dr. Harold sitting in front of the group, begins to speak "Good morning everyone, glad to see everyone here, well almost everyone" He then looks over at Mike grinning.

"Today I have a colleague coming in to sit with the group today, he should be walking in any minute".

The doors to the rec room then begin to slowly open, Dr. Harold looks over at them, and says "Oh here he is now, please Welcome Dr............

The End

Mike and Dr. Bachman will return in Diagnosis: The Sanitarium